DO YOU KNOW
WHAT I'LL DO?

DO YOU KNOW WHAT I'LL DO?

by

CHARLOTTE ZOLOTOW

Pictures by

GARTH WILLIAMS

HARPER & ROW, PUBLISHERS

DO YOU KNOW WHAT I'LL DO?

Text copyright © 1958 by Charlotte Shapiro Zolotow
Text copyright © renewed 1986 by Charlotte Zolotow
Illustrations copyright © 1958 by Garth Williams
Illustrations copyright © renewed 1986 by Garth Williams

Library of Congress catalog card number: 58-7755
ISBN 0-06-026930-8
ISBN 0-06-026940-5 (lib. bdg.)

TO MY SISTER
Dorothy Arnof

One day a little girl
said to her little brother,

Do you know what I'll do
when the flowers grow again?

I'll pick you a bunch and you'll be happy.

Do you know what I'll do
when it snows?

I'll make you a snowman.

Do you know what I'll do
when it rains?

I'll catch the rain in a pail for your plants.

Do you know what I'll do
when the wind blows?

I'll put it in a bottle
and let it loose when the house is hot.

Do you know what I'll do
at the seashore?

I'll bring you a shell
to hold the sound of the sea.

Do you know what I'll do
in the city?

I'll buy you a surprise.

Do you know what I'll do
at the movie?

I'll remember the song and sing it to you.

Do you know what I'll do
in the night?

If you have a nightmare
I'll come and blow on it.

Do you know what I'll do
at the party?

I'll bring you a piece of cake
with the candle still in it.

Do you know what I'll do
on my walk?

I'll look at the clouds
and tell you the shapes when I get home.

Do you know what I'll do
when I wake up?

I'll remember my dreams and tell them to you.

Do you know what I'll do
when I grow up and am married?

I'll bring you my baby to hug.
Like this.

DATE DUE			

25489

E
ZOL

Zolotow, Charlotte.

Do you know what
I'll do?